EVERYWHERE
FACES
EVERYWHERE

Also by James Berry

For young readers:

Picture Books:

EVERYWHERE
FACES
EVERYWHERE

Poems by James Berry

With illustrations by Reynold Ruffins

Simon & Schuster Books for Young Readers

ACKNOWLEDGMENTS

Poems previously published in books by James Berry:

from *Chain of Days*
Just Being
Night Comes Too Soon
Calabash Tree
Thinking Back on Yard Time
Nana Krishie the Midwife
Goodmornin Brother Rasta

from *Isn't My Name Magical?*
Happenings
Occasion

In anthologies:

Bits of Early Days, *New Writing*
Rain Friend, *Ten Banana More*
Trick a Duppy, *Classic Poems to Speak Aloud*
Coming of the Sun, *Longman's*

SIMON & SCHUSTER BOOKS FOR YOUNG READERS
An imprint of Simon & Schuster Children's Publishing Division
1230 Avenue of the Americas, New York, New York 10020

Book design by Lucille Chomowicz
The text for this book is set in Garamond 3.
The illustrations are rendered in black ink and cut paper.
Printed in Hong Kong
10 9 8 7 6 5 4 3 2
Library of Congress Catalog-in-Publication Data
Berry, James.
 [Playing a dazzler]
 Everywhere faces everywhere :poems / by James Berry ; with illustrations by Reynold Ruffins.
—1st ed.
           p.   cm.
 First published in Great Britain by Hamish Hamilton under the title: Playing a dazzler.
 Summary: A collection of poems exploring the diversity found in a childhood in Jamaica and
later observations of young people in England.
 ISBN 0-689-80996-4
 1. Children's poetry, Jamaican. 2. Jamaica—Juvenile poetry.
3. England—Juvenile poetry. [1. Jamaica—Poetry. 2. England—Poetry.
3. Jamaican poetry.] I. Ruffins, Reynold, ill. II. Title.
PR9265.9.B47P53 1997
821'.914—dc20 96-30301

CONTENTS

**for
Myra Barrs
and her contribution
to education**

INTRODUCTION

Not long ago, where difference and variety abound, English literature mostly celebrated only a small picked-out choice of human life and experience. Now we are more and more enjoying the benefit of a wider, fuller, truer variety of our human situations in print. In a natural way young readers are also sharing in this. It seems that many of the pieces here may well fall into this "new" material category.

Everywhere Faces Everywhere is a book of poems with subjects drawn from my Caribbean childhood and my grown-up work in the United Kingdom. Over the many years here, I have gone invited into schools numberless times to read my poems and stories to classes of children and teachers and to lead writing workshops.

For the section Bits of Early Days, I looked back into my Caribbean childhood and found some of these poems. "Night Comes Too Soon" comes from my toy-making evenings with other children out-of-doors. And we did not like to give up our busywork when night came down and stopped us. Yet, "For Meeting Four-Weeks-Old Eve," like "This Carry-on of Two Boys Over Kim," "Playing a Dazzler," "Occasion," and "A *Sad Sad* Nick" and "Absent Player"—which are poems about games played alone or absentmindedly—all have been inspired by children in the U.K. Again, the "Boy Don Rap" idea came from my watching and listening to a Caribbean village boy reciting and performing his own made-up rap poems. I so enjoyed his happy, wishful poems that took him into a wider and more adventurous world, I made up my poem like one of his.

The section Look, No Hands obviously celebrates nature generally, especially through the sun, with magical things that sunlight does. I can't at all account for any writing model or any suggestion that prompted "Ritual Sun Dance." And yet I do recognize how its idea and form have a kind of African-style resemblance. This celebration of the sun—using a mock-fear that the sun may not return and should be pleaded with—does make me wonder. And, I see "Rain Friend" and "Good Morning Brother Rasta" merely as varied nature poems.

Generally, the section Trap of a Clash brings together poems of conflict and the consequences of people being left out of sharing in the needed and good things of life. It is "Saying Hello—New Style," which is dedicated to a mixed-race Caribbean poet friend living in the U.K., that redeems these pieces with suggestions and hope of new possibilities.

Again, the section Watching a Dancer features my two-culture self. "Village Man Hot News," with his walkabout announcement, like "Nana Krishie the Midwife," an old lady I visited on a return to my home village, "Poetry Find in Caribbean Proverbs: 8 and 9," and "Haiku Moments: 2," all carry Caribbean culture material. At the same time, "Retirement Poem" marks and praises the service of a teacher in England—someone I worked with many times. Also, my going into some London schools, and becoming absorbed by a new school population of different racial faces, inspired "Everywhere Faces Everywhere."

The Fish and Water Woman section uses my childhood memories of known mystery and myth. These share company with funny and satirical characters drawn from Caribbean-London's yearly street carnival. Then, last of all, living here in this section, too, is what that mystery and magic of love is like.

Children's lives seem to express a particular kind of childhood culture. This child culture fills children and absorbs and drives them with activities to find more and more of the self, physically and mentally. I hope something of a poem or two here may excite and contribute even a little pleasure to that young reader's culture.

—James Berry

BITS OF EARLY DAYS

BITS OF EARLY DAYS

Still a shock to remember
facing that attacking
dog's fangs and eyes at its gate.
Seeing our slug-eating dog come in
the house, mouth gummed up, plastered.

Still a joy to remember
standing at our palm-fringed beach
watching sunrise streak the sea.
Finding a hen's nest in high grass
full of eggs.
Galloping a horse barebacked
over the village pasture.

Still a shock to remember
eating with fingers and caught
oily handed by my teacher.
Seeing a dog like goat-hide flattened
there in the road.

Still a joy to remember
myself a small boy milking a cow
in new sunlight.
Smelling asafetida on
a village baby I held.
Sucking fresh honey from its comb
just robbed.

Still a shock to remember
watching weighted kittens tossed in
the sea's white breakers.
Seeing our village stream dried up
with rocks exposed
like dry guts and brains.

Still a joy to remember
walking barefoot on a bed of dry leaves
there in deep woods.
Finding my goat with all of three
new wobbly kids.

Still a shock to remember
facing that youth-gang attack and all
the needless abuse.
Holding my first identity card
stamped "Negro."

Still a joy to remember
walking fourteen miles from four A.M.
into town market.
Surrounded by sounds of church-bell
in sunlight and birdsong.

(asafetida—a strong smelling gum resin twisted into a
baby's hair to encourage good health.)

HAPPENINGS

One thing happens
another thing happens.
A cup slips, it falls,
it crashes into pieces
The cat leaps, she rushes,
she bangs herself through the cat door.
"*CAAAW!*" a Crow says, sitting
in the treetop at the garden fence.

One thing happens
another thing happens.
An apple drops from its branch.
It rolls, it stops; a dry leaf
holds it, like a saucer.
"*SEEE, SEEE, SEEE, SEEE!*"
a strange bird screams,
sitting there in the apple tree.

One thing happens
another thing happens.
Wind lifts off a lady's hat.
It flies, it swirls, it dips,
it falls in the park pond.
A small dog leaps into the water, gets the hat
and gives it to the lady.
A big Boxer who watched goes deep-voiced,
"*WOW WOW! WOW WOW!*"

FOR MEETING FOUR-WEEKS-OLD EVE

You are with us, Eve—
arrived among the leaves
to the cooing of mum and dad
saying: *welcome welcome* Eve—
new face among the leaves.

And, worshippers,
we bring more smiles, more gifts,
more coos, more one-way talk.
We tell whose eyes
and nose and mouth you have—
new face, Eve, among the leaves.

You are put to bed, picked up,
pushed around in your carriage.
Soon, your voice will be there
in the school-playground noise.
And you wall-bounce your ball.
Soon again, you start up, you drive
your own four-wheels—
new face, Eve, among the leaves.

You are growing *now*.
And your ways now of sleeping,
crying, feeding, looking, smiling,
trusting, touching, wishing, sleeping,
all will be the same,
differently stated only,
through your days, days and days—
new face, Eve, among the leaves.

Like your soft self
may your tough self always meet
our worship of you now
saying: *welcome welcome* Eve—
new face among the leaves.

THIS CARRY-ON OF TWO BOYS OVER KIM

"Kim and me make one;
anybody else makes none."

"Kim and me heat up a room."

"Kim knows you aren't dumb cos you don't know better,
you're dumb cos you don't matter."

*"Kim knows your type scatters
dustbins at old people's doorways."*

"Leave off that *Kim Kim* from a rotten tongue."

"Kim's eyes are hypnotists."

"Kim's voice sets me up a chuckling idiot."

"Kim's warm lips shut me up."

"Her round hips turn me on to stutter."

"Her armful of waist turns me on to worship."

"Mind I don't scatter your teeth like a smashed cup!"

"Mind I don't dislodge your face!"

"If you don't know, our
regular haunts happen twosome."

*"If you don't know, after our recent fling
she took my secret engagement ring."*

"When high tide swept away her bathing costume
I took her home dressed in moonlight."

*"You, in Kim's plans—
you pimply face pig, you stink!"*

"You are dumbstruck, on the ground: Kim and me fly
upside down, two hundred miles an hour, roller coasting."

*"You leave Kim alone!
Or get yourself missing, stiff, on the dump site."*

"You leave Kim alone.
Or risk a left arm with everything right!"

"Mind! Mind you don't hide, rotting."

"Look! There goes Kim.
Kim—arm-in-arm with Tim!"

PLAYING A DAZZLER

You bash drums playing a dazzler;
I worry a trumpet swaying with it.

You dance, you make a girl's skirt swirl;
I dance, I dance by myself.

You bowl, I lash air and my wicket;
I bowl, you wallop boundary balls.

Your goal-kick beat me between my knees;
my goal-kick flies into a carriage-and-baby.

You eat off your whole pound-chocolate cake;
I swell up halfway to get my mate's help.

My bike hurls me into the hedge;
your bike swerves half-circle from trouble.

I jump the wall and get dumped;
you leap over the wall and laugh, satisfied.

I touch the country bridge and walk;
you talk and talk.

You write poems with line-end rhymes;
I write poems with rhymes nowhere or anywhere.

Your computer game screens monsters and gunners;
my game brings on swimmers and courting red birds.

OCCASION

On, on—it's on.
The music stings, the music bites.
The roomful breaks up body shapes.
And everybody is a bobbing head here.
Everybody is a mover everywhere.
Beat mover Danny is a blue-jeaned rocker;
Gill in Superman-shirt is a reggae pulser.
Oh, making a hop of it, we are rocking it.
Isn't this all we ever want to do?

Arms come. Arms go. Sounds are hot.
Legs go astray, all crazy, the lot.
Disorderly bodies get in a muddle;
other hips move with a good firm wiggle.
Gary dances in a tiger-head shirt;
Sue does hers in a flared red skirt.
Oh, rock it! Writhe! Stamp it! Jump!
Isn't this all we ever want to do?

Each one a scatterbrained music fool,
everyone is mad, but everything's cool.
Two girls dance together, in purple jumpsuits;
Barry moves alone in his white sneaker boots.
Mark wants to cling;
Jane breaks it and does her own trotting.
Oh, music! You are such a twitch maker!
Isn't this all we ever want to do?

On, on—it's on.
Fat legs and thin legs prance about;
Sonia mouths the music with a curled mouth.
And all in our carnival of colors
just go on like real carnival revelers
with nobody, nobody, wanting to stop
in this on and on with this hot, hot, hop
in having all one say—
"Oh, every day, let us have a friend's
                    HAPPY BIRTHDAY."

BOY DON RAP

I am the boy they call Boy Don,
well known as the number one style man
with only that bother of a sister
and each of the others called brother.
But I done them in with new-craze:
I leave them in old-time days
the way me one wear my cap
with the style of rap.
        Everywhere people like to see me;
        everywhere people like to hear me,
        this boy they call Boy Don:
        the number one style man.

I do it, live it, hype up my name.
Say, I fly a spacecraft: get more fame.
Get eyes fixed on the moon
going, going, footprinting it soon.
Then show, I am more than a hoot:
I walk round the world barefoot.
And for sweet landing on the bum
I do the highest high jump.
Everywhere people like to see me;
everywhere people like to hear me,
this boy they call Boy Don:
the number one style man.

And making heself this big little joy
is only Boy Don this big little boy
swimming the ocean with a whale,
never letting go of its tail.
Then, apron on, doing a dish,
he makes up some escoveitch fish.
And see him there in the kitchen
you don't believe he's one of the children.
Everywhere people like to see me;
everywhere people like to hear me,
this boy they call Boy Don:
the number one style man.
The number one style man.

(escoveitch fish—Jamaican pickled fish)

A *SAD SAD* NICK

    Truly, truly to me, to me—
not to my sisters—
they carried on. On and on.
Don't slide down the banisters.
Don't slide down. Don't, don't
slide down the banisters. Don't.
I jumped halfway down the stairs.
And how could I, could I see
our carpet color dear old cat,
"Velvet," was there, snoozing,
to get her guts gushed out
guzzled up, like stringy, mushy tomatoes?

ABSENT PLAYER

Ball games her agony,
at rounders she was posted out
and placed at the furthest
possible position
under a tree almost.

Lost, as usual, dreaming,
she heard some vague panic noises
breaking through, as if, desperate,
the whole team were shouting,
"Catch the ball! Catch the ball! Catch it!"

She slowly turned her face upwards.
She did not see the ball,
but, it aimed at a resistance
and came down straight, smack
onto a well-shaped mouth.

Her front teeth were loosened
in blood. She lay on the grass.
No way could she tell any
sympathy from boiling rage
around her. She cried, quietly.

SHARING IS AN OPEN GAME

Cricket ball runs errands
teasing out a game
teasing out hands together.

Judgments not behind doors,
fair or unfair or good or bad,
a verdict is there
open to sky, field, pavilion.

In the shades of global faces
players come onto the scene.
Eyes and hands go crazy
after a runabout ball.

All of an art in it
with moneymaking in it
movements in body balance act
consume to consummation
to wild applause and shock
and silence and heartache.

And in popular strike of ball,
in crafted flight of ball,
new professors arrive, graduated
in seeing all sides *clear clear*

while entranced in the dance
with that wood and leather,
wooing that drive that tells
a game is never truly lost or won.

A game played is
a field with scattered sounds
of musical instruments
taking part in a fusion.

THINKING BACK ON YARD TIME

We swim in the mooneye.
The girls' brown breasts float.
Sea sways against sandbanks.

We all frogkick water.
Palm trees stand there watching
with limbs dark like our crowd.

We porpoise-dive, we rise,
we dog-shake water from our heads.
Somebody swims on somebody.

We laugh, we dry ourselves.
Sea-rolling makes thunder
around coast walls of cliffs.

Noise at Square is rum-talk
from the sweaty rum bar
without one woman's word.

Skylarking, in our seizure,
in youthful bantering,
we are lost in togetherness.

Our road isn't dark tonight.
Trees—mango, breadfruit—all,
only make own shapely shadow.

Moon lights up pastureland.
Cows, jackass, all, graze quietly.
We are the cackling party.

CHILDHOOD TRACKS

Eating crisp fried fish with plain bread.
Eating sheared ice made into "snowball"
with syrup in a glass.
Eating young jelly-coconut, mixed
with village-made wet sugar.
Drinking cool water from a calabash gourd,
on worked land in the hills.

Smelling a patch of fermenting pineapple
in stillness of hot sunlight.
Smelling mixed whiffs of fish, mango, coffee,
mint, hanging in a market.
Smelling sweaty padding lifted off a donkey's back.

Hearing a nightingale in song
in moonlight and sea-sound.
Hearing dawn-crowing of cocks, in answer
to others around the village.
Hearing the laughter
of barefeet children carrying water.
Hearing a distant braying of a donkey
in a silent hot afternoon.
Hearing palm trees' leaves rattle
on and on at Christmastime.

Seeing a woman walking in loose floral frock.
Seeing a village workman with bag and machete
under a tree, resting, sweat-washed.
Seeing a tangled land-piece of banana trees
with goats in shades cud-chewing.
Seeing a coil of plaited tobacco
like rope, sold, going in bits.
Seeing children playing in schoolyard
between palm and almond trees.
Seeing children toy-making in a yard
while slants of evening sunlight slowly disappear.
Seeing an evening's dusky hour lit up
by dotted lamplight.
Seeing fishing nets repaired between canoes.

CHILDREN'S VOICES

Caves of bats crisscross
under sky of open dusk.
Fowls crouch in with leaves.
Cows call their pent calves.

Flame tree is quiet, like a hill
carved into a colorful umbrella.
Shouts and laughter clap round
night shaded fruits hanging
and animals grazing.

Children will go on
flinging wide their last
shrieked fun to stars, and delay
that interfering break of sleep.

NIGHT COMES TOO SOON

Here now skyline assembles fire.
The sun collects up to leave.
Its bright following paled,
suddenly all goes. Dusk rushes
in, like door closed on windowless room.
Children go a little sad.

Fowls come in ones and groups
and fly up with a cry
and settle, in warm air branches.
Tethered pigs are lounging
in dugout ground.

Muzzled goat kids make muffled
cries. Cows call calves locked away.
Last donkey-riders come homeward
calling, "Good night!"
Children go a little sad.

Knives-making from flattened
big nails must stop. Kite ribs
of tied sticks must not develop.
Half shapes growing into bats
and balls, into wheels and tops
must cease by night's veto.

And, alone on shelves, in clusters
on the ground in corners, on
underhouse ledges, these
lovable embryos
don't grow in sleeptime.
Children go a little sad.

Bats come out in swarms.
Oil lamps come up glowing
all through a palm-tree village.
Everybody'll be indoors
like logs locked up.
Children go a little sad.

LOOK, NO HANDS

LOOK, NO HANDS

Without muscles, without an arm or hand grip,
look how I, wind, bend back trees' big limbs.

Without wheels, without a down-hill,
look how I, the sea, roll and roll along.

Without a hurt, without a bruise,
look how I, waterfall, tumble down rocks.

Without bricks, without hammer or nails,
look how I, tree, build a house for birds.

Without apprenticeship, without hardware store,
look how I, eagle, build my family's nest.

Without getting even one single penny,
look how we, apple trees, give up our red apples.

Without a hose, without a sprinkler,
look how I, sky, water gardens with my rain.

HAIKU MOMENTS: 1

1
Stems and leaves downy,
hidden here white under stone,
to be green sunlight.

2
Ouch! tongue! lime juice knifed,
needled, scalded, bitten, with
this charged sunlight sting!

3
Still *hot hot* fanning—
wish I stood barefeet in one
big field of new snow!

4
Mango—you sucked from
sunrise to sunset to be
this ripe scented flesh.

5
Settled in the bowl
alone, banana lies there
cuddle-curved, waiting.

COMING OF THE SUN

The sun came out in England today—
faces cracked wanting to smile.
Overcoats were guests overstayed.
Nakedness wanted to be the rage.

The sun came out echoing on:
people yearned for distant coastlines
and yearned for all good news;
neighbors stood at fences, asking.

The sun came out in England today.
Lambs leaped over each other on hillsides.

RITUAL SUN DANCE

O sun O sun—
noon eye of noontime breath
makes blooms come,
unfolds big trees from seeds,
stirs crusts into leaves,
dresses cold shapes *warm warm*—
excite the little grown
to be fully grown.
    Hey-hey! Hey-hey!
    Sun gone down. Gone down underground.
    Come dance, come dance!
    Don't mind who father is.

Don't mind who mother is.
Come dance and see the sun come back!

O sun O sun—
kisser who tickles crusts,
who swells yams in the ground,
fattens up droopy reeds
like apples and plums
like bananas and mangoes,
like sharp spices sharper—
touch everywhere.
    Hey-hey! Hey-hey!
    Sun gone down. Gone down underground.
    Come dance, come dance!
    Don't mind no child, no herd.
    Don't mind your sound of words.
    Come dance and see the sun come back!

O sun O sun—
flood-flame of air,
making pods pop
making seeds drop,
grass growing to strong rum,
oranges getting brighter,
grapes getting sweeter—
drape fields, drape fields.
    Hey-hey! Hey-hey!
    Sun gone down. Gone down underground.
    Come dance, come dance!
    Don't mind what roof house is.
    Don't mind what kind dress is.
    Come dance and see the sun come back!

O sun O sun—
mighty dazzler
who moves the zero hour,
who moves the zero hour—
make nuts brown,
brushless,
noiseless.

    Hey-hey! Hey-hey!
    Sun gone down. Gone down underground.
    Come dance, come dance!
    Don't mind what track leads you.
    Don't mind what wheels bring you.
    Come dance and see the sun come back!

THATCH PALMS

Small settlement of Thatch Palms,
here beside the sea,
I come to see you.

Living in turbulent face of the sea,
umbrella leaves shadow clifftop.
Trunks all straight and smooth,
roots grip rocks like ironclaws.

An old tree is a standing pole,
bare of limbs,
time and wind beheaded.

I pick up
a dropped broad leaf:
so well ribbed
it flies from my hand
like a kite
into the sea.

I hug
a living tree.
I wonder at
the straightness
of Royal Palms
and at
the plumed show
of Queen Palms
and at
the timeless crops
of Date Palms.

I remember
monkey face
of fallen coconuts
will burst
into growth
after months
at sea, drifting.

And people go
from here
and knit palms
into roofs
and brooms
into hats
and mats
into baskets
and novelties.

I wonder at
the guardian
stance of palms.
I wonder at
their beginning.

I wonder at
the stubborn nature
of the fanlike leaves.

RAIN FRIEND

All alone out-a deep darkness
two mile from Aunt Daphne
little Dearie—knee high little Dearie—
come push door open,
sodden with rain to hair root
all through to thin black skin
from naked foot bottom.

And she stand up there giggling.
A-say she did like the sea
the sky throw pon her,
coming down all over her
like say all her friends in it too
running about pasture and dark trees.

And when she did close her eyes and laugh
she hear Cousin Joe jackass braying
and Great House dog them barking
and road-water carry and carry her
like she a sailing boat in darkness.

GOOD MORNING BROTHER RASTA

Good-days wash you mi brother
a-make peace possess you
and love enlightn you
a-make you givin be good
and you evermore be everybody
a-make Allness affect you always
and you meetn of eye to eye be vision
and all you word them be word of wonderment

TRAP OF A CLASH

TRAP OF A CLASH

Noise of two dogs alarms like ten.
A terrible tussle and tangle here.
A swopping of bites and yelps
as dogs brace each other, up on back legs.
They fall, busy with attack—
all in a panic—
with tossing heads vicious
with quick yap-yaps for bone crush
with bared ripper teeth snarl fixed
with a grab for a grab
with jaw-grip for jaw-grip through flesh.
Each one in a trap, in a struggle.
Neither can let the other go.
Hurt, cries, terror, hold them
till now. Torn and punctured enough
they split. One goes
off home with a limp,
the other with a sorrowful whimper.

CHILD-BODY STARVING STORY

Head misshapened and patchy with hair
    with shocked eyes in a hole with a stare

cheeks collapsed in skin among bones
    with cracked lips having not one moan

ears keeping a nonstop whining sound
    with neck hardly more than a broom-handle hold

hunched up shoulders v-shaped
    with twiggy arms claws-fingered

a belly all self pumped-up
    and knees the knotted marbles thinly skin wrapped

legs the drumsticks knee-knockers
    with feet not finding a body to carry together—

show me off, as this body-exhibit labeled,
"A NOT-ENOUGH-TO-SHARE LEFT-OUT"
and other times labeled,
"A GOVERNMENT'S NON-CARING LEFT-OUT."

EMPTINESS CHILD-BLUES
for every girl and boy with no-dinner

You come home from school
little less a fool.
You see no little food.
You say, what's the good?

Table and cupboard empty.
Whole-yard empty.
Fireside dead.
And nothing is said.

No little sugar—
I'm to have ashes-and-water?
No one crumb of bun—
I'm to eat dirt baked in hot-sun?

Boy, this here time
is a real devil time—
wanting to make dry bone
of people and home.

And doesn't come by wheel or foot.
Hardtime just comes and takes root.
Comes and doesn't ask.
Never helps a single task.

So leaves are rusty.
The place is all dusty.
Rivers have dried up and gone
with people trying to go on.

Hear what I say, eh!
Hear what I say, eh!
a thin-ribbed jackass is going to rock
everyone a skeleton man to work.

BUSH ACCIDENT MESSAGE

Mummah Mummah and Buddy and Sis
Dear-Dear break her leg

her *clean clean* young-girl leg
up at Highrock Pass

After she didn get far
her load go fall on her

O she drop down "biff"
pop her leg like a stick

like a somtn a load-up donkey mash
and flesh and bone pop-up with the mash

Dear-Dear break her leg
Lord her *clean clean* young-girl leg

and they bringin her droopy
O bringin her droopy
on Mister Mack donkey

GRANNY BEGS DAUGHTER JANIE

Janie! Janie. Don't!
Please. *Don't* beat Boysie!
Pile in no more knocks.
More rocks on him, this is.
Do. Please. Don't.
Badness well schooled him.
It's others you beat through him.
Our boy. With all-time hurt.
Our boy. With shirt patchy-patchy.
    Stop the beating!
    Janie. Janie. Stop it!

Dear Janie. Miss Janie.
Please. *Don't* beat Boysie!
Remember. He's short of a dad.
Short and short. No father.
Lacks reared him. He swelled and swelled
for overdoses of good.
Not force. Not force and battering.
    Stop the beating.
    Janie. Janie. Stop it!

Dear Janie. Miss Janie.
Enough. Enough!
Don't drive him in with crooks.
We'll try coaxing him with books.
No more pain in this young frame.
Give more coaxing. No more hitting.
No more getting him knotted.
We want him heartened. Heartened.
We want him *so so* heartened!
    Yes. Yes. Give me Boysie.
    Boysie? Our one-day big man Boysie?

OTHER SIDE OF TOWN

Talking faces
Wear the blues
Of singing faces

Thoughtful faces
Wear the blues
Of vocal faces

Laughing faces
Wear the blues
Of sad faces

Hopeful faces
wear the blues
Of hopeless faces

Dressed up faces
Wear the blues
Of poverty faces

Sober faces
Wear the blues
Of drunken faces

Praying faces
Wear the blues
Of swearing faces

Love-swoon faces
Wear the blues
Of hate-struck faces

Clean free faces
Wear the blues
Of jail faces

O other side of town
Your sad faces
Are blues faces

OKAY, BROWN GIRL, OKAY

For Josie (9 years old, who wrote to me
saying . . . "boys called me names
because of my color. I felt very upset . . .
My brother and sister are English. I wish I was,
then I won't be picked on . . . How do you like
being brown?")

Josie, Josie, I am okay
being brown. I remember,
every day dusk and dawn get born
from the loving of night and light
who work together, like married.
 And they would like to say to you:
 Be at school on and on, brown Josie
 like thousands and thousands and thousands
 of children, who are brown and white
 and black and pale-lemon color.
 All the time, brown girl Josie is okay.

Josie, Josie, I am okay
being brown. I remember,
every minute sun in the sky
and ground of the earth work together
like married.
 And they would like to say to you:
 Ride on up a going escalator
 like thousands and thousands and thousands
 of people, who are brown and white
 and black and pale-lemon color.
 All the time, brown girl Josie is okay.

Josie, Josie, I am okay
being brown. I remember,
all the time bright-sky and brown-earth
work together, like married
making forests and food and flowers and rain.
    And they would like to say to you:
    Grow and grow brightly, brown girl.
    Write and read and play and work.
    Ride bus or train or boat or airplane
    like thousands and thousands and thousands
    of people, who are brown and white
    and black and pale-lemon color.
    All the time, brown girl Josie is okay.

ROCK AGAINST RACISM

for Jo Beneba

Born here and come to her sixteenth year
She felt lifted from threat and despair.
People her time with her fill the park
All through the afternoon on to dark.
In youth music bright like the banners
With the soulful crowd-pleasing singers
All were bonded like branches swaying
Stating, hating is not fun.
And safety holds like a chain all one.
  She swayed with the thousands to and fro:
  Yeah, yeah, to the future we go.
  Past, now, future, take stock
  This is London London Rock.

Togetherness like a familiar house
Unlocks her hopes in this beat of pulse.
England-born Black in her coming out year—
Can she rely on this banished fear,
All this shake-up to conquer old dread
To bring in a new human way instead
With whites in from all round Britain's towns
Bonded with blacks, yellows, and browns?
Hating is not fun.
  She swayed with the thousands to and fro:
  Yeah, yeah, to the future we go.
  Past, now, future, take stock
  This is London London Rock.

Badges of Rock Groups cry out up front;
Straight and pin-and-patch styles cry consent:
We condemn that hate—
That hate at sight of a different shade.
Drunk as mystics for a new age,
Rockers rocked wanting a *new new* bridge
Halfway from England
Halfway from Africa-land.
And safety holds like a chain all one.
    She swayed with the thousands to and fro:
    Yeah, yeah, to the future we go.
    Past, now, future, take stock:
    This is London London Rock . . .

INNERCITY YOUTH WALKS AND TALKS

He walks along with me and talks.
Says, Yes. I'm a full-time
graffiti artist, and busy
with a real job what I like.

Says, My style's my own style.
All artists know my work
and could get my message
on wall, in train, in bus,
on chimney, lamppost,
drainpipe, pavement, wherever.

He says, I baffle heads of the town
with strategic secret signs.
Gives me a real buzz that.
Indoors sitting down.
How my art strikes people
just for the look at it.

Satisfaction work that,
Takes art to the public.
Makes you vegetarian.

For a lift inside and a cool
my dad settled on "the weed."
For a lift inside and a cool
I look for fresh work ideas.
To hide from faces
my dad lives in dark glasses.
To hide from faces, I took up
my nighttime secret work.

Yes, he says. Risk of the job is
the risk of any job.
A work with height and depth
keeps eyes open round the head
for rail repair men coming
or light of train dashing up
and keeps you nippy as a rat.

Says, My mom took to a wig
to look like Tina Turner.
Mister Big my brother swears
nobody likes him
and he's stuck with that.
My dad doesn't get a pay,

doesn't get praises,
respect or adventure.
I make art in danger places.
And it's a buzz traveling daytime
seeing my secret signs everywhere.

Says, Everybody has a downside.
My downside takes to height.
Nobody in my family took to art.
Why not go for it I said.

Says, Managed big gold buckle belt
with head of African king on it.
But I want a Suzuki bike
and can't manage it.
So I go for getting grimed
in city rubbish in corners.
Getting stuck between walls.
But, it's a satisfaction work.

ACTION IMAGES

Hairy dog shakes mud from itself;
parrot flies to pieces from shelf.

Girl dressed in high heels of odd pairs;
Mom and Dad fall downstairs in tears.

Fat boy pinpricks blown-up balloon;
cat leaps high from trouble in room.

Tall thin man sits on neighbor's fence
shouting: "Neither for nor against!
Neither for nor against. . . !"

SAYING HELLO–NEW-STYLE
(in this difference that became John Agard)

Looking slender like a sapling
he arrived there and stood
handing out steel-drum sounds
all printed bright on bunting
to be put up as road signs.

And here was saying hello—new-style.
You guess two tribes in one, hand-waving
to fox, bird, city bowler-hat:
"Good day, compañero! Please,
hear a violin-and-drum sound."

And you should know a hidden brown eye
with a hidden blue eye, acute
with a grapevine and an airwaves ear
working one seeing
with the same message.

From the *wide wide* gestures
apples and mangoes rain down
in a flutter of poems
like colorful leaves, to classrooms
of children, collecting, laughing.

You know sounds charged, possessed,
taking up whole stage,
in dizzy movements
in spins of yarns
in release of songs.

You know now
a busy worker
teasing out new singing
till an audience looked
everybody felt sparkling.

You see, a different look
does not mean "switch-on for war."
And you know
a deep-feeling spreeboy,
time-picked for laughter-making.

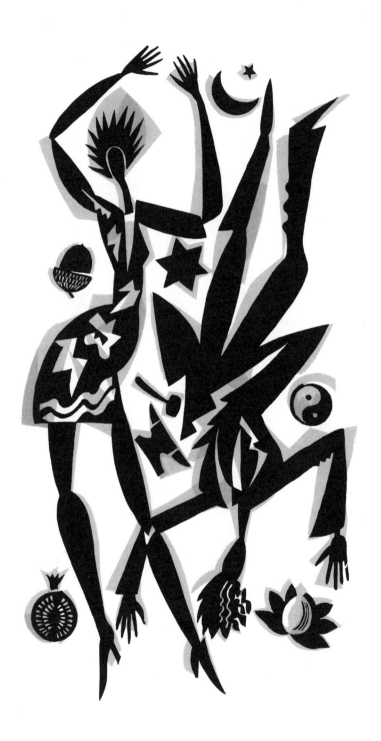

WATCHING A DANCER

WATCHING A DANCER

She wears a red costume for her dance.
Her body is trim
and shapely and strong.

Before she begins
she waits composed,
waiting to hear the music start.

The music moves her.
She hears it keenly. The music
pulses her body with its rhythms.

It delights her. It haunts her body
into patterns of curves and angles.
She rocks. She spins.

She stretches entranced. She looks
she could swim and could fly.
She would stay airborne from a leap.

Her busy head, arms, legs, all know
she shows how the music looks.
Posture changes and movements are

the language of the sounds, that
she and the music use together
and reveal their unfolding story.

VILLAGE MAN HOT NEWS

Tonight—jumpup!
Jumpup tonight!
Dance!
Dance up at Johnmariddle house.
Johnmariddle win thousn pound.
Johnmariddle board and grass a-suffer tonight.
Warman nod-nod with he big guitar.
Tonman rumble bass-fiddle like drum.
Little Cita a-sing.
Rum. Ice. Jerk-pork. Patty.
Come dance to moon till mornin soon!

Tonight—jumpup!
Jumpup tonight!
Dance!
Dance up at Johnmariddle house.
Johnmariddle win thousn pound.
Capital-K beat drums like he a-beat racehorse.
Wailerman trumpet a-streak moonshine.
Whole-a-yard of moon a-shake up.
Sol-o honey sax groan.
Rum. Ice. Jerk-pork. Patty.
Come dance to moon till mornin soon!

(jerk-pork—barbecue pork)

NANA KRISHIE THE MIDWIFE

So keen on me those old eyes
the tracked black face
flowed with light

The tongue and gum ladled
stubborn words remembering
how I the boy child had knocked
thirty years before and hustled her
to come to the little cottage

Come with owl's wisdom and red
calico bag of tricks
to end labor: snap
and smack a newborn to cry

And now she looked at me surprised
and not at all surprised I had
come back from abroad
looking in a widened range
out of miracles she used and knew
time had discredited

For her ancestor's knack
her tabooed secrets now worked
in books of others
as ancient practices

Dreaming in her illiterate life
I felt the faltering tones
her startling shivered voice
thanking God
for showing me ever so well

RETIREMENT POEM

for teacher, Maisie Carter

Years after years
and years after years
she wakes with shoes on
and goes
hugging books, pens, folders,
off to scatter words
in the growing of girls and boys.
Will she kick her shoes off now?

EVERYWHERE FACES EVERYWHERE

Again fascination holds me.
In a London innercity classroom.
Holds me in these shades of eyes
around me in faces
plum-blue to nutmeg-brown,
melon-gold to peach-pale.
From nearby districts here.

The young gather
with old symbols of
the Anvil and the Acorn
and the Golden Stool
and the Egg and Lotus
and the Crescent and Star
and the Pomegranate
and the Star of David
and the Yin and Yang.
Different knowings have worked their ways
towards different seasonings.

I am in wonder. My own days at school
returned always with only
our all-similar flock of faces.

I am centered on this togetherness
of children. Who ocean-crossed differently.
Who were a mystery of strange blooms.
Who were like missing parts, of a circle,
that simply arrived. And no official,
no ministry, no boardroom, planned it.

I look up—considering.
This old stone building here.
Its imperial coffer-share.
Is this how inheritors are made?

Is time showing me
a little movement
of human growing?
Through secret workings
of the left hand? While
the ever busy right hand
hammered, hammered, fixing?

(Anvil—Nordic symbol, meaning creation.
Acorn—Nordic symbol, meaning long life.
Golden Stool—Ashanti gold stool: symbol of unity.
Egg and Lotus—Hindu symbol of health and eternity.
Crescent and Star—Islamic religious symbol.
Pomegranate—Semitic symbol, meaning abundance.
Star of David—symbol of Judaism.
Yin and Yang—Chinese symbol of balance in the
creation principle.)

POETRY FIND IN CARIBBEAN PROVERBS: 8

1: Never pull out your insides
   and give them to a stranger then
   take dry leaves and stuff yourself.

2: Trouble catches a man
   a child's clothes will fit him.

3: Trouble never blows conch shell
   when it's coming.

4: Tiger wants to eat a child, tiger says
   he could swear it was a cat.

9

1: Afraid of a frog
   you'll run from a crab.

2: Sugarcane knows how to trap
   sugar from sun and raindrop.

3: Fire and water are friendly
   together, a home is there.

OWN-MADE PROVERBS

1
Plant a seed you could have a tree.

2
Trees make mangoes; man makes wheels.

3
Want to see a horse cross-legged
in a chair, tell its mane is blonde hair.

4
Want to swallow a whale start at the tail.

5
Who'd want food or friendship
without pepper, salt or pickle?

6
Can't expect to take a pig to bed
and have everybody saying nothing.

7
Night-riding a bicycle you should
twinkle on starry bright.

FISH AND WATER WOMAN

FISH AND WATER WOMAN

We would see that mermaid.
Three of us came. We waited.
Nobody had seen her.
But village people talked about
the mermaid's habits.

At middleday, she comes out
and sits there on the flat chalk stone
combing her long golden hair, shining.

Five minutes she sits. Combs her hair
in the mottled sunlight. Then, gently
she slides and pushes herself
back to the dark deep pool to sink
and swim away, into the rocky watery cave.

Early early we came. We waited. Concealed
against the mango tree's trunk, beside
the wall of a rock and the pool.
Excited, but silent, we huddled closely.

And all through this waiting was
the going-on of bird songs,
branches rubbing and squeaking
and sifted sunlight sprinkling us.
Then, to shake us up, we saw
middleday had come!

Shadow tips of tall bamboo trees touched us.
And, a truth we disbelieved followed:
a mango dropped noisily in the pool.
"She's here! Mermaid's coming."
All of us whispered, "Yes. She's here!"
Our breathing changed, ready to choke us.
Bodies rigid, eyes on flat stone,
we watched. We listened.
Why didn't we hear a body
dragging itself out of water!

And, together we agreed, endless
time had passed. And somebody sighed.
"Missed her. We missed her. Wonder how?"

We heard the gentle gurgle of water falling
and heard the flutters and songs of birds
and felt the strong sun-hot of afternoon
that filled our clothes and heated our skin.

"Next time. Next time. We *will* see her!"

SONG OF WHITE-PEOPLE GHOSTS

Why don't you come with me—
come on with me and see
red face duppies in a picnic feast
under cotton tree—
under cotton tree!
in a middleday sun-hot?

Why don't you come with me—
come on and hear and see
pretty talk in a tittle-tattle
to fork-plate-and-spoon tinkle-tinkle
under cotton tree,
in a middleday sun-hot?

Why don't you come with me—
come on with me and see
ladies taking pin eat peas
all dainty-dainty if you please
under cotton tree!
in a middleday sun-hot?
    In a middleday sun-hot?

(duppies—ghosts)

TRICK A DUPPY

If you wahn trick a duppy
and wahn walk on *happy happy*
in a moonshine—bright moonshine—
hear how and how things work out fine.

You see duppy. No whisper. No shout.
Make not the least sound from you mouth.
One after the other *straight straight,*
strike three matchsticks alight.
Drop one then two of the sticks ablaze
and before you walk a steady pace
flash dead last match like you drop it
when *smart smart* it slipped in you pocket
to have duppy haunted in a spell
and why so you cannot tell.

But duppy *search search* for third matchstick
to vanish only when 6 a.m. come tick.

Note on the poem "Today's People Carnival Picked"

The most important part of this title—Today's People—is based on the kind of costume-ideas used by group players of London's yearly Notting Hill Caribbean Street Festival.

So "Today's People" is an idea based on the revelers who "play Mas" at Carnival, dressed in costumes representing human, animal, or imagined characters. At the same time, importantly, it is also the title of each group of players. It is shown in bold lettering mounted on the group's float that carries their costumed musicians playing and parading in heightened performance.

Players supporting a band "play Mas" dressed in costumes representing characters of their band's theme. Names of characters are brightly shown on costumes. And these characters usually get created with their beautiful, comic, or ugly sides well stressed outlandishly for entertainment. And all this can again be played up conspicuously as the players dance behind their float, with all its accumulated spectacle, parading with its band.

—James Berry

TODAY'S PEOPLE CARNIVAL PICKED

"MAN ENTANGLED WITH SPINNING WHEELS"
rocks beside "GIRL IN HIGHEST HEELS."
Cool mover "BLOKE STREETWISE"
dances with "BIRD OF PARADISE"
while "JUDGE OF OLD BAILEY"
prances with "COY LADYFAIRY"
and strutting of "DAZZLING PEACOCK"
moves with "JUST A PATCHWORK FROCK."
And "A WOMAN DRESSED IN IRON"
rocks along with "MAN IN LION."
    In this world and sometimes out,
    crowd-rocking is a shout
    of costumed revelers
    behind a costumed band
    pulsing, pulsing, along
    in Carnival.
                CAR-NI-VAL!

Watch the jogging of "GIRAFFE"
how she is calm with "OWN CALF"
and jumping about of "MISTER FOX"
is for "CHICKENS MESHED IN AND BOXED"
while a sweaty and grinning "WARTHOG"
dances hot for "COOL BEAUTY BAG."
In jitters "TERROR STRICKEN TURKEY"
is with "SHARPENED CUTLERY."
And "ALL FOR LIVING SAKE"
rockes cautiously with "SNAKE."

> In this world and sometimes out,
> crowd-rocking is a shout
> of costumed revelers
> behind a costumed band
> pulsing, pulsing, along
> in Carnival.
> > CAR-NI-VAL!

Watch how that "SLICK GUN-CARRIER"
moves cockily with "WATCHFUL TIGER"
while cross looking "RAGS WITH A FROWN"
is halfhearted with "MAN GROWN DOWN."
Offended "OLDE WORLDE GEAR"
jumps up angrily with "LATEST FASHION GEAR"
while slow easy moves of "PANDA"
go with slow trots of "ZEBRA."
And a wooed "SLICK SERPENT"
is dignity itself with "CITY GENT."

> In this world and sometimes out,
> crowd-rocking is a shout
> of costumed revelers
> behind a costumed band
> pulsing, pulsing, along
> in Carnival.
> > CAR-NI-VAL!

See how man "BY PROFESSION ARTY"
is a dance of scorn with "GRAFFITI"
while the jigging of "DEBUTANTE"
is with showy "TEDDY THE-RAVE-AND-RANT."
Strick rhythm of "GIRL STEADY-ROCK-STEADY"
moves along with "SOLID MAN FRIDAY."
Hot-hot overworking "BADDY"
dances with stiff "BEJEWELLED LADY."
And busy feet of "SWINGING PALMS AT NOON"
skip *happy happy* with "LAUGHING MOON."

    In this world and sometimes out
    crowd-rocking is a shout
    of costumed revelers
    pusling, pulsing, along
    in CAR-NI-VAL!
                CAR-NI-VAL!

HAIKU MOMENTS: 3

1
Here along roadside
yellow of gorse announces
sunlight is coming!

2
Stopped here listening—
this heedless grind of traffic
staggers the birdsongs.

3
To benches, to grass,
offices fall out for lunch—
sunlight's on London!

LOVE IS LIKE VESSEL

Love is like vessel
that is Mother and is Father
and is nature parts
that become pure water.

Love is like face of ground
kissing feet
under whatever
bodyweight it greets.

It is like elements
that together make night
and elements
that together make light.

It is like carrying
a head that makes no weight
and also like quiet warmth
around cold hate.

Love is like finished work
with mixes so well wed
that grain, milk, yeast, heat are balanced
offering a *fine fine* bread.

Love is like roundness
of a running wheel
over a bumpy road
or one simply smooth like steel.